W0313760

Billy THE Kid

Also by Michael Morpurgo

The Dancing Bear
The Butterfly Lion
Farm Boy (also illustrated by Michael Foreman)
Dear Olly
Toro! Toro!
Cool!
Private Peaceful

For younger readers

Albertine, Goose Queen
And Pigs Might Fly
Jigger's Day Off
Martians at Mudpuddle Farm
Mossop's Last Chance
Mum's the Word
Mr Skip

Picture books

Sam's Duck
Wombat Goes Walkabout
The Gentle Giant

Audio

Kensuke's Kingdom (read by Derek Jacobi)
Farm Boy (read by Derek Jacobi)
The Dancing Bear (read by Sir Ian McKellan)
The Butterfly Lion (read by Virginia McKenna)
Dear Olly (read by Paul McGann)
Out of the Ashes (read by Sophie Aldred)
Billy the Kid (read by Richard Attenborough)
Private Peaceful (read by Paul McGann)

michael morpurgo

The Billy Kid

ILLUSTRATED BY

MICHAEL FOREMAN

TED SMART

This edition produced for The Book People Ltd,
Hall Wood Avenue, Haydock, St Helens WA11 9UL

First published in Great Britain in 2000 by Pavilion Books Limited
This edition published by Collins 2002

Collins is an imprint of HarperCollins*Publishers* Ltd,
77-85 Fulham Palace Road, Hammersmith, London W6 8JB

The HarperCollins website address is www.harpercollins.co.uk

5 7 9 8 6 4

Text copyright © Michael Morpurgo 2000
Illustrations copyright © Michael Foreman 2000

ISBN 0 00 769324 9

The author and illustrator assert the moral right to be identified
as author and illustrator of this work.

Printed and bound in Great Britain by
Clays Ltd, St Ives plc

Conditions of Sale

This book is sold subject to the condition that it shall not be lent, re-sold, hired out or otherwise circulated without the publisher's prior written consent in any form of binding or cover other than that in which it is published and without a similar condition including this condition being imposed on the subsequent purchaser.

For Francis and Nan.
MM

For my sons Jack, Ben and Mark
and all fans of the great game.
And for Gianfranco Zola.
Thanks for the memories.

MF

I shouldn't be here really, not by rights. I should've been pushing up the daisies a long time ago. But I'm not. I'm here, and I'm eighty years old, eighty years old today. One way or another I've been a lucky old beggar. I've got my eyes, my ears – all right, they may be a bit on the fuzzy side, but they work – and I think straight, most of the time. Of course, the old knee gives me a lot of grief, but it always has done, ever since the war anyway… I'm used to it.

Can't complain, not on a lovely day like this.

Tenth of April and I'm sitting on my favourite park bench under my favourite tree, a great spreading chestnut tree. And the bees are out. Lovely. I've got my picnic on my lap, and there's a bunch of kids playing football. What more could I want? One of them's good too, skinny like I was, a bit scrawny, little bandy legs, but he leaves them all standing. Like I did, once.

I think the boys are going to put on a bit of a birthday party for me tonight. I've got to be back by six at the latest – that's what they said. I'll do my best, but it's Chelsea against Liverpool, and I'm not missing a single minute of it, party or no flipping party. I couldn't sleep last night, I never can before match days. Too wound up. I've always been like it. "It's only a game of football, Billy," – that's what the boys keep telling me. But it's more than that. A lot more. I know I should've given up by now, but I haven't. When it comes to football I'm like a little kid, like those kids over there in the park, the same park I scored my very first goal – that'd be well over seventy years ago now.

Dad sometimes got tired in the afternoons, and had to go and lie down, then I'd practise by myself up against the brick wall – with both feet. Dad always made me do it with both feet. He told me two things I've never forgotten: that if I wanted it badly enough I could be the best footballer in the land, and that I must never go fighting in a war, any war. I tried

to do what he'd told me, but things didn't quite work out the way he'd have wanted. The sun was shining that day too, but it was cold, and Battersea power station was belching smoke out of its chimneys. My dad was standing there

watching me score my very first goal. We went off to the Chelsea match afterwards – against Preston North End – and Chelsea lost, but that day I didn't mind, neither of us did. Happy as a lark I was, and so was my dad. He carried me all the way home on his shoulders. He never said much, he never did, but he was proud of me that day, I know he was. "One day," he said, "One day Billy, you could play for Chelsea. All you've got to do is work at it." And I believed him.

That's what my dad did for me, and then later on Ossie – Mr Osborne from school. They gave me self-belief, and that counts for just about everything in this life. If you haven't got that, you haven't got anything, and I should know. Like that scrawny kid out there I was a natural. I had a lucky gift. For a start I was nippy. I was best out on the wing, the right wing. No one could catch me out there. I was faster than all the kids twice my age. And somehow I could always make a football do whatever I wanted it to. It just came easy to me, I don't know why, but it did.

We always kept the special football on the shelf in the kitchen greased up so it wouldn't crack. Dad had brought it back from France when he came home from the First World War. He'd found it in the mud on the Somme – the only good thing he ever brought back from that war, that's what he told me. The trouble was that he'd brought something else home as well – gas in his lungs. I can remember his cough better than I remember his voice. Sometimes he'd be coughing his heart out all night long, and I'd lie there listening in the dark and crying because I could hear how it was hurting him.

I grew up knowing him a lot better than I knew my mother. He couldn't go out to work on account of his lungs, so we were together a lot. Mum would take in washing and be working all day every day, to keep the wolf from the door; and then she had my little brother Joe to look after as well. Dad and me played football for hours on end – in the street, in the park, in the back garden, anywhere. I was only allowed the special football at weekends and even then only when it was dry. He didn't want it getting wet. We played with a tennis ball. Dad said if I could do it with a tennis ball, then a real football would be "easy-peasy".

Only a few days after I scored that first goal out there in the park, my dad died. Suddenly there was no more coughing in the house. Mum let me carry his football to his funeral. I held her hand all the way through. For the first time it was me holding her hand, not the other way round. We buried him in Putney churchyard, down by the river. It was a grey day. He always loved the river. We'd often go feeding the ducks down there, then we'd sit and watch the boats go chugging by. So it was just the right place for him. You've got to be in the right place when you're dead, that's what I think. I mean, after all, you're dead for a long time, aren't you? I greased the football up when I

got back home and put it back up on the shelf in the kitchen, and that's where it stayed. I never kicked it again after that.

I grew up quick after Dad died. We missed him, of course we did; but there wasn't time to go all tragic about it. For a start, Mum had another baby on the way. There was little Joe to look after and school to go to, and the washing to fetch and carry for Mum. But every spare five minutes I'd be out the back with my tennis ball, shooting or heading or trapping or dribbling. And I never missed a match day at Chelsea, not if I could help it. That was why I turned professional, sort of, at the age of eight – to pay for my ticket. But then I got caught. And that was how Ossie came to be my coach – in a roundabout sort of a way.

Emmy was just born. Mum needed every penny she could earn from taking in washing to keep us all fed and clothed, so I knew I couldn't ask her for money. If I wanted to go to the match, then I had to earn it somehow, or steal it. Ossie said it was stealing, but it wasn't, not really. It was just a bet – a bet I knew I'd win, but a bet just the same. In break-times I'd dribble a tennis ball from one end of the school playground to the other, and there was a farthing in it for anyone who could take the ball off me – one at a time and no fouling – and a farthing to me if they couldn't. They all knew I was good, but they all fancied their chances. Nine times out

of ten I'd manage it. I'd send them one way and go another, or push it through their legs, or just dribble round the outside of them. It was easy pickings, and I always had enough for a ticket at the Shed End on Saturdays – I'd always gone in the Shed End with Dad, right behind the goal. My favourite spot in the whole world – still is.

One morning I was called out of lessons and sent to Ossie's room. I could see straight away that he was none too pleased with me. He told me I was a gambling good-for-nothing scallywag, that it was as good as taking money out of other kids' pockets, as good as stealing, he said; and he wouldn't have stealing in his school. Then he told me to bend over. Three whacks he gave me. Didn't hurt that much, not really. And afterwards, just as I was going out, he said: "Now that's over and done with, Billy, there's something I want to say to you. I've been watching you. You're young, but you're good, good enough to be in the school team already. More than that, I think one day you could be very good – maybe. But if you want to be the best, you've got to be more than a fancy dribbler. I can coach you if you like, help you along a bit."

And he did. He most certainly did. Ossie took over where my dad had left off. Three, four times a week, in all weathers, we'd be out practising, me and the rest of the school team, and Ossie kept us at it. He'd lay his handkerchief down in front of goal and we'd have to cross the ball from the wing so it landed spot on. And he'd run the legs off us too, tire us out. "Clever isn't good enough, Billy," he'd tell me. "You've got to be tough with it." It was Ossie that made me tough, who taught me to think football, to know what was going on around me and on the other side of the pitch; and it was Ossie who went to my mum and paid for my first pair of proper football boots. We hardly ever lost a match. And if I didn't score in every match he'd want to know why. "You've got to be hungry, lad, goal hungry," he'd say.

Most of the others were eleven and I was still only eight, but I wasn't too cocky about it – they made sure of that. They'd slap me down good and proper if I got any airs and graces. Besides, they liked having me there because I'd score goals, lots of them; and like me, they liked winning. I was a sort of lucky mascot for them. "Billy the Kid," they called me. If we won three matches on the trot, Ossie would take us all to see Chelsea, and he'd pay for the lot of us. He may have whacked me from time to time, but Ossie had a heart of gold, a real heart of gold.

That bandy-legged kid out there, he's got it, he's really got it. Balance, ball control, grit, he's got the lot – just like Stanley Matthews, Jimmy Greaves, Georgie Best, and that Michael Owen. Head right over the ball, knows just what he's doing without even thinking about it. But he needs to look up more, look around him, know what's going on. He's not looking.

Sausage rolls. Just how I like them, crisp and flaky. I'll have one to keep me going. Lovely. Mum used to do sausages on Sundays. Toad in the hole and bubble and squeak and gravy. Loved her sausages. Loved her gravy. Loved her.

My boots have got a bit muddy. I polished them this morning too. That's the only trouble with the park. Still, who's looking?

Little Joe always scuffed his shoes at the toes, and tore his trousers out at the knees. Mucky little chap he was, never wiped his nose or washed his face unless Mum made him. But he was always a chirpy sort, big too and healthy. He grew fast. By the time I was fourteen and he was twelve, he was already as big as me. More like a twin he was. Real good chums we were.

Emmy was never well, not really, not after the

whooping cough. She nearly died of it. Mum sat up with her night after night till she got better. She lived for us kids. She didn't spoil us, nothing like that – she could be strict enough if she had to be. She fed us, clothed us, kept us warm – I don't think she ever had a thought for herself. She only ever had one luxury – lavender. She always smelt of lavender. Once a year we'd all go down to the seaside for a week, at Broadstairs, and stay with her sister, Aunty Mary. We loved it down there – the beach, the boats and the donkey rides. Emmy loved donkeys. She always wanted to bring one home with her and she'd cry buckets when she couldn't.

Summer of 1935. I was fifteen, and we were just home from Broadstairs when Ossie called at the house. He had something important to discuss, he told us. Mum sat him down and gave him a cup of tea. He'd been talking to Mr Knighton, the manager at Chelsea Football Club. It turned out that Ossie was a Chelsea scout, that he'd recommended me to Mr Knighton and Mr Knighton had seen me play and would I sign forms for Chelsea? Twelve and sixpence a week and all the football I wanted to play. I'd be cleaning the players' boots, keeping the ground spick and span, but there'd be a place in the Chelsea side in a few years' time, if it turned out that I was good enough. What did we think? I could have hugged him. Mum took it all very calmly. She sipped her tea and put her cup down slowly. "Well," she says, "it'll be up to Billy to decide of course, but I think that sounds most acceptable." Most acceptable! She always had a way with words did my Mum, bless her. The very next day I kicked my first football at Chelsea Football Club, and cleaned my first pair of boots too.

I was like the cat that had got the cream. I couldn't believe my luck. None of my school chums had found work – there wasn't much about, not in those days – and here I was, being paid for what I loved doing best.

There was a whole bunch of us lads who started on the ground staff at Chelsea that September, and all of us lived and breathed football. There was a lot of skivvying; but we didn't mind, none of us did, because the rest of the time we got to practise, and sometimes with our heroes too – the first team. Best of all was when Burgess or Mills or Sam Weaver – the skipper he was – or Hanson, would come and kick a ball about with us.

I got a bit of a shock in the early days when I found there were others just as fast as me, stronger than me and every bit as determined too. I was used to playing with bigger lads of course, but these lads were good, and the trouble was that as the years passed I didn't seem to be getting much bigger. "Legs like sticks of celery,"

that's what Mr Knighton the manager said, and he wasn't far wrong. I knew that if I was to have any hope at all I had to build up my strength and my speed. So Ossie would take me out for training in the park each evening when I got home. Joe would often come along too and practise with me. I could see how proud he was of me and that made me want to practise all the harder. It was thanks to them, as much as anything, that I held my own at Chelsea, despite my size. By the time I was seventeen I was selected for the Chelsea Reserves side – on the right wing, where I belonged, where I was best.

The first match I ever played for Chelsea Reserves was against Arsenal Reserves. There weren't many there to watch, but Mum came, and Joe and Emmy and Ossie, and they saw me score two goals. One was a simple enough tap-in. The other I really enjoyed: a dribble in towards goal, slipping the ball through the legs of one defender, round another and a little chip over the goalie. I can still see the look on his face as the ball floated over his head and into the goal – horror, disbelief, despair all in one. Lovely.

I was in the newspapers the following day. 'Billy the Kid bamboozles the Arsenal'. For the whole of the next year I was a regular in the Chelsea Reserves, and a regular in the newspapers too. I didn't think life could get better. But it did – for a while at least.

1939 began as the best year of my life. Towards the end of that football season I was picked for the first team. Twelfth of March 1939, just a month or so before my nineteenth birthday, I trotted out in my Chelsea shirt for the very first time. I was on cloud nine, seventh heaven. We were playing Preston North End away, and we lost, badly. No one was looking at me, that was for sure. I was awful, leaden-legged and useless. Ossie, who came to all my matches, took me on one side afterwards and said I had to forget the shirt, forget who I was playing for, where

I was playing, all that, and just play my game.

When we played Sunderland the next week at home, it was like I was in the playground again at school, or out in the park with Joe. I ran rings round them, laid on a couple of goals and scored one myself. That was the first time I heard the crowd at the Shed End chanting my name – "Billy, Billy the Kid! Billy, Billy the Kid!"

It sends warm tingles down my spine even now just to think of it. Before the season ended three weeks later I had scored seven more goals and all the papers were saying I'd be playing for England within the year. One paper called me 'Billy the Wonder Kid'. Another said I was 'as good as Stanley Matthews, maybe better'. It would have gone to my head a lot worse than it did, if it hadn't been for Ossie.

"Don't read all that stuff, Billy," he told me. "Don't even look at it. Not good for you. Let your mum cut it out and stick it in a scrapbook. You can read it later when you're older – can't hurt you then."

Mum did put it all in a scrapbook – she was always taking it out and looking at it and showing it – but it disappeared, like everything else.

That summer Mum married again, married Ossie – and I never even saw it coming. Joe and me were both 'best men', and Emmy was the bridesmaid. So the man who'd whacked me at school, who had taught me most of my football, who had been like a father to me since Dad died and a real friend to the family too, became my second father. It couldn't have been better. It was a great day for all of us, confetti everywhere and a huge wedding cake made like a football pitch in Chelsea-blue icing. And then they went off to Broadstairs for a week's honeymoon.

They were still away on the third of September when war was declared – another thing I hadn't seen coming. I'd been too busy with my football to worry about what was going on in the world outside. To start with the war didn't seem to matter that much anyway. Not a lot happened. What did the newspapers call it, 'the phoney war' or something?

Then suddenly in our house it wasn't phoney

at all. Joe made up his mind that he ought to go and join up. He'd be seventeen in a month and he'd join up as soon as he could. I thought he was joking at first. We all did, but he wasn't joking at all. He was so determined about it, and so sure he was right too. It was simple, he said. Hitler was evil, just plain evil. He'd invaded Czechoslovakia and Poland. What was to stop him from coming over and invading England if we didn't fight him? Mum said he was far too young to go, so did Ossie. And I told him that our dad wouldn't have wanted it, how he'd warned me never to go to war. I told him what I believed too, that it could never be right to kill another human being, no matter what. We had our first big blazing argument. He wouldn't listen, not to me, not to anyone. It was his life, he said, and he'd live it or lose it the way he wanted. The argument went on and on. I said terrible things I can't forget; and he said terrible things too, things I can't forget either – about how he'd always looked up to me, until now, about how all I wanted was to play my lousy football and to hell with the rest of the world. It didn't come to fisticuffs, but we weren't far off. In the end we just stopped speaking to each other.

One morning Joe upped and left without telling anyone; and the next we heard from him was from a training camp on Salisbury Plain. He wrote Mum a card. He'd be off to France soon, he said, and sent lots of love to all of us. He came home on leave once, but I was away, playing football. Mum told me he looked really grand in his uniform, that I should be proud of him. Deep down I was too, but I just could not bring myself to say it or tell him. I never wrote to him. He never wrote to me.

In the dark days of 1940 we listened to all the news broadcasts we could. Everyone did. The news from France was worse every day. The army was surrounded and being driven back to Dunkirk. There were thousands and thousands of men on the beaches, all the army we had, and a whole armada of little boats was going over to pick up as many as they could. There were pictures in the newspapers of the soldiers being helped off the ships, wounded, bedraggled, beaten. After that it looked like invasion was a dead certainty.

Then the telegram came. Joe had been killed at Dunkirk. Only Emmy cried. The rest of us just sat there in the kitchen with the clock ticking, Ossie with his arm round Mum, each of us all

alone with our sadness. I went out after a while and sat in the park on this very same bench and wept like a baby. I joined up the next day, I couldn't stay out of it, not now, not any more.

The squirrels here are as tame as you like. I've had them right up on the bench with me before now. They don't come for love, just food – I know that. There's one sitting by my boot right now, but he's not having any of my sausage roll,

no matter how much he makes eyes at me. There were squirrels about the day I joined up, chasing each other up the trunk of that oak tree by the park gates. A branch came off that one last winter. Smashed the bench below into little pieces. He's washing his nose now. I like it when he does that. All right, have a bit of sausage roll, just a little bit. Greedy little beggar.

Chelsea tried to stop me. Mr Knighton told me I had a great future in football and that football would go on somehow, war or no war. But Mum didn't even try to talk me out of it, nor did Ossie. They understood. I joined the Royal Army Medical Corps. I'd be driving ambulances, working in field hospitals. This way at least I'd be doing something for Joe – that's what I thought, that's what I told myself.

So I found myself in khaki, and running up hills in full battle order, and learning how to march, and turn left, and turn right and about turn, and swing my arms in time with everyone else. I learnt to shoot a .303 rifle and a Bren gun, and how to bayonet a stuffed dummy. I learnt how to polish boots too, army boots this time, not football boots. Then we ran up more hills, lots more, until we'd completed our basic training.

Before they sent me off to war six months later they'd taught me how to drive an ambulance, how to dress wounds, put on splints for broken bones, take temperatures, carry stretchers. I never had much time to play football; but I did think of it, and I missed it too, the excitement, the roar of the crowds, all of it. The boys knew who I was of course, and ribbed me a bit to begin with, but they soon forgot all about that. And so did I.

I was Billy again, not Billy the Kid. The football part of my life was over. I tried to put it out of my mind. I'd pick it up again where I'd left off when the war was finished and done with. I only had one leave before I was sent overseas, and in a way I wished I'd never gone home. Joe was a photo on the mantelpiece now, and Mum was tearful every time she looked at me. "She's frightened of losing you as well," Ossie told me just before I left.

Emmy gave me her little gold cross to keep me safe, and hugged me as if she'd never let go. I walked away from her, from all of them, and took the train down to Southampton to join the troop ship. We knew we were going to the North African desert, but we didn't know where, not exactly. It was my first time on a ship and, to begin with, I hated it. I kept thinking of the submarines lurking under the sea – I couldn't swim either.

But I soon forgot about the submarines. Someone had made a football out of rags, and word had got about the ship that I was 'Billy the Kid' from Chelsea. For a few hours every day we'd play football up on deck, a kind of football

anyway, and I could forget about where I was, and what I was going to. But in the evenings alone on deck with just the sea and the sky, I'd talk to Joe. I talked to him a lot. I've always talked to Joe ever since, specially when I need him, mostly when I'm very sad or very happy.

We landed at Tobruk in pitch darkness, and drove the convoy of ambulances off into the desert. We could hear the rumble of the guns, see the whole night sky lit up ahead of us – like a terrific thunderstorm it was, but with no rain. Then the sun came up over the desert, big and red, and we saw what sort of place we'd come to. Nothing but rocks and sand as far as the eye could see, and

hundreds of our soldiers streaming past us, retreating back towards Tobruk, on foot, in lorries. We set up our field hospital right beside the road where the wounded were waiting, sitting on the sand in their hundreds. Only a stone's throw away from them, the dead were lying in rows waiting to be buried. They lay so still. It was my first day of war – and my last, as it turned out.

We spent that morning burying the dead. None of us spoke. We just dug and cursed the flies that wouldn't leave us alone. I was sick a good few times – and it wasn't on account of the heat. It was hot by now, burning hot, hot enough someone said to fry an egg on your helmet. More and more wounded were being brought in all the time. The sound of the guns was coming closer all the while now, and then we heard the chattering of machine gun fire.

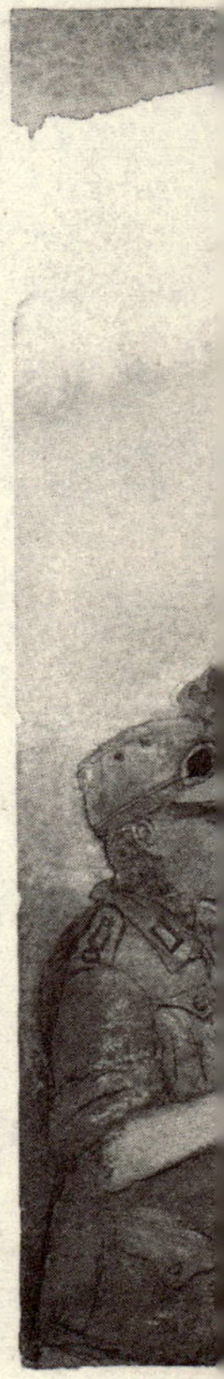

That same evening we got the order to pull back. We were stretchering the wounded into the ambulances when a German armoured column came roaring and clanking towards us out of the desert. They never even bothered to stop, but just waved and rattled on by. The infantry came behind them. There was a bit of shouting, but no shooting. They just rounded us all up and marched us off. No one marched in step now. We didn't swing our arms together either. All that had been for nothing. I was a prisoner-of-war.

There were thousands of us POWs, maybe thirty, forty thousand, all sat around in the desert, guards wherever you looked. Not that anyone was going to run off. Where to? Tobruk had fallen to the Germans, and there were hundreds of miles of empty desert on one side and the sea on the other. For three days we sat there, no food, no water. I'd never been so thirsty in all my life. At night we froze, in the day we roasted. Then they marched us back into Tobruk – which was full of very happy-looking Germans. From there they shipped us off to Italy.

It was on the ship that I first bumped into Robbie, who turned out to be a lifetime Chelsea supporter. Once he recognised me he looked after me like I was his little brother. All the way up Italy in that stifling train, packed in like cattle –

four days it took – he saw to it that I had enough water and food to keep me going. And when at last we found ourselves marched into a prisoner-of-war camp, somewhere north of Venice, he was there right beside me, almost as if he was protecting me from the guards. And Robbie was a big man, about as broad as he was high. I felt well protected. We slept in the same hut too, and as the months passed we became the best of mates. And we stayed that way.

We didn't get our first letters for months, and some of us got very down about that. Robbie, always the chirpy one – he reminded me of Joe sometimes – did his best to keep my pecker up, but I took it hard. It was the wire all around us closing me in, the lousy food they gave us, the cold in the winter, just the endless days that dragged on with no news, and no hope of any news.

When I was alone I'd talk a lot to Joe and tell him my troubles – that helped. I kept thinking how stupid I'd been, how I'd just walked off the troop ship and into captivity, how I'd let everyone down.

I used to have this dream that I was back home and the crowd was doing their chanting: "Billy, Billy the Kid! Billy, Billy the Kid!" And I'd score a goal and Joe would come running onto the pitch from the Shed End and clap me on the back and I could see in his face that he was so proud of me. Then I'd wake and I'd know I was in the hut. I knew it by the smell of it: wet clothes, wood smoke and unwashed men. I'd lie there in the dark of the hut, and think of home, of Joe, of football.

Once the letters came I felt much better, for a while. Lots of them came at once – we never knew why. But it was good just to hear that Mum and Ossie and Emmy were all right, that they were still there, and I wasn't alone in the world. There'd been some bombing in London, so they'd sent Emmy down to Aunty Mary's in Broadstairs for a while. She sounded very different in her letter, very grown up somehow. She told me how she wanted to go back home, but that Mum wouldn't let her, how Aunty Mary fussed over her and how she was fed up with her. She told me she had decided she was going to be a nurse when she was older. I read the letters over and over again, and wrote home whenever I could. Those letters were my lifeline. The next best thing in the world were the Red Cross parcels. How I looked forward to them – marmalade, chocolate, biscuits, cigarettes. We did a lot of swapping and bartering after they came.

I'd swap my cigarettes for Robbie's chocolate – never did like smoking, just not my vice – I did my best to end up with mostly chocolate. It lasted longer, if I didn't get too greedy.

As for the Italians guarding us – there were two sorts. You had the kind ones, and that was most of them, who'd pass the time of day, have a joke with you; and then the others, the nasty ones, the real fascists who strutted about the place like peacocks and treated us like dirt. But what really got me down was the boredom, the sameness of every day. I had so much time to think and it was thinking that always dragged me down, and then I wouldn't feel like doing anything. I wouldn't even kick a football about.

It was partly to perk me up, I reckon, that Robbie came up with the idea of an F.A. Cup competition. He organised the whole thing. Soon we had a dozen league sides – all mad keen supporters only too willing to turn out for 'their' club back home. I trained the Chelsea team, and played centre forward. Robbie was at left back, solid as a rock. For weeks on end the camp was a buzz of excitement. Everyone trained like crazy. Suddenly we all had something to do, something to work for. What some of us might have been lacking in skill and fitness, we made up for in enthusiasm. The Italians laughed at us a bit to start with, but as we all got better they began to take a real interest in it. In the end they even volunteered to provide the referees.

I was a marked man of course, but I was used to that. I got up to all my old tricks, and the crowd loved it. Robbie was thunderous in his tackling. Chelsea got through to the final, against Newcastle.

So in April 1943, under Italian sunshine and behind the barbed wire, we had our very own F.A. Cup Final. The whole camp was there to watch, over two thousand men, and hundreds of Italians too, including the Commandatore himself. It was quite a match. They were all over us to start with, and had me marked so close I

could hardly move. Paulo – one of the Italian guards we all liked – turned out to be a lousy ref, or maybe he was a secret Newcastle supporter, because every decision went against us. At half time we were a goal down. Luckily they ran out of puff in the second half and I squeezed in a couple of cheeky goals. Half the crowd went wild when I scored the winner, and when it was all over someone started singing 'Abide With Me'. We fairly belted it out, and when we'd finished we all clapped and cheered, and to be fair, the Italians did too. They were all right – most of them.

Next day came the big surprise. Paulo came up to me as I was sitting outside the hut writing a letter. "Before the war I see England play against Italia in Roma," he said. "Why we not play Italia against England, here, in this camp?"

So there we were a couple of weeks later on the camp football field facing each other, the best of us against the best of them. We all had white shirts and they had blue – like the real thing. Paulo captained them, I captained us. They were good too, tricky and quick. They ran circles round us. I found myself defending with the back four, marshalling the middle and trying to score goals all at the same time. It didn't work. They went one goal up soon after half time and were well on top too for most of the second half. We really had our backs to the wall. The crowd had all gone very quiet. We were all bunched – when the ball landed at my feet. I was exhausted. All I wanted to do was boot it up field, just to get it clear. But I had four Italians coming at me and that fired me up. I beat one and another, then another, and leaving Paulo sprawling, made for

their goal. I had just the goalie to beat. I feinted this way, that way and stroked it in. It was the best goal I ever scored. The whistle blew for full time. I was hoisted up and carried in triumph round the camp. We hadn't won, but we hadn't lost. Honours even. Just as well, I've always thought. Both sides could laugh about it afterwards. Important that.

Some months later, we could all see that the Italians were becoming more and more twitchy. The nasty ones were getting even nastier. Something was up, but we didn't know what, not really. Paulo did try to warn us.

"Things no good," he told me one day. "We Italians, we no want this war. Is no good."

I thought he was just being friendly,

but it turned out to be more than that. One morning we woke up and the guards had just vanished, leaving the gates wide open behind them. Some of us thought it was a trap, but then an Italian farmer came up to the camp gates in his horse and cart and told us. Italy was out of the war. "We are friends now," he said. "Go, go quick. Soon Germans come. Go quick."

So two thousand of us just ran for it into the countryside of Northern Italy. None of us had any idea where to go, not to start with. We just wanted to get out while we had the chance. Robbie and I made for the mountains. We thought we'd be safer up there.

We had a week of wonderful, almost carefree freedom. The country people were kind to us wherever we went and fed us. We couldn't make ourselves understood, nor understand much of what they said, but we got by. One old bloke gave us a map of Italy, and seemed to be saying we'd be better off going south because the Americans and British had landed in the south, and that the Germans would be coming down from the north any day. He was right about that. The very next day we saw a German column winding its way down the valley. We were already cut off from the south. It was Robbie's idea to head for France, that maybe we could link up with the French Resistance and find our way back home through neutral Spain, over the Pyrenees. So we began our long trek west, through the hills of Italy, walking by night, and resting up by day.

The swallows are back. I saw my first one only the other day, dipping down in the puddle in the vegetable garden. He's building in the woodshed, just like he did last year. I suppose he's the same one. Swallows always come back to the place they were born – that's what they say. Come to think of it, that's what I did too, in a roundabout sort of a way.

There were swallows overhead that day too, hundreds of them skimming the river. We'd been on the run for a couple of months by now, maybe more, and we were tired, tired right out, and hungry, and thirsty too. We'd been hiding up in the woods all day and had just come down to the river for a drink, when this old woman came along the river bank carrying a basket of washing. She took very little notice of us at first, but when she'd finished her washing she beckoned us over. She never said a word, but led us up a track through the woods, and out onto the open hillside beyond. The farmhouse looked more like a hut from the outside, but on the inside it was spotless. She sat us down and fed us – soup, hot soup. Lovely. Best soup I ever had. Nothing was said, except our thankyous.

That same evening we heard the jangle of cow bells outside, and a girl's voice calling. Then she came in. She looked surprised, but not frightened.

She looked at us and then at her mother, and as the two of them spoke her eyes never left us. And I couldn't stop looking at her either. She was the most beautiful girl I had ever set eyes on. Lucia. I've only got to think her name and her face comes back, a face I'll never forget, not as long as I live. In all the time we knew each other we scarcely said a word, but she'd smile and I'd smile. We held hands, that's all. I remember she had rough hands, rougher than I thought they'd be. And she laughed at my sticking up hair. They looked after us for weeks, until we were strong again and rested and ready to go on. We'd sleep in the house at night and go into the woods by day,

just in case the Germans came.

Then one evening they did come. We heard them from the woods. There was shouting. Robbie and I crouched down at the edge of the wood. We saw it all. One of the soldiers was waving my battle dress jacket in their faces and screaming at them and slapping them. They stood side by side and said nothing, arms linked, Lucia hiding her head in her mother's shoulder.

The soldiers just shot them up against the barn wall, and the sound of it echoed around the mountains. It was my jacket that did it, my jacket that killed them. We reached France in the end, more by luck than by judgement. We hadn't a clue where we were going, not really. We kept to the wild country, the high country, sleeping rough, always going west, living off the land, begging what food we could, stealing it sometimes when we had to. But we were always hungry.

The people were kind, and brave too. Nine times out of ten they'd give us something to eat, and we knew now what terrible risks they were taking.

All this time Robbie looked out for me as best he could. He'd never let me take chances. It was always him who went knocking on doors for food, while I waited out of sight until he was quite sure it was safe. He was brimful of kindness, that man. I'd never have made it without him.

One night, lying there under the stars, we were asking each other what we most looked forward to. "Toad in the hole," I told him. "What about you?"

"I want to wake up in the morning at the Shed End, Billy, and watch you bamboozle the Arsenal again."

When we woke the next morning we were still on our hillside. And crouching all around us was a bunch of wild looking men, some in berets, all of them armed to the teeth, and not at all friendly. Maquis, they called themselves, resistance fighters. They took us to their camp high up in the hills, and there we found dozens more like us, all escapees from Italian camps. We felt a bit like prisoners again – there was always someone keeping an eye on us. They fed us and made us as comfortable as they could – but I think we were a bit of a nuisance. They had more important things to be doing. Soon enough, they said, they'd be taking us down to the Americans who had landed in Southern France, then we could go home. And that's what happened.

So there I was on yet another ship, this time going from Marseilles to Liverpool, back home. When we landed they gave us a week's leave.

Robbie and me came to the parting of the ways. He went north to Aberdeen to see his wife who was in the Land Army up there, and I went south to London. We said we'd keep in touch, but we never did.

I could have sent a telegram home, but I didn't. I thought I'd just walk in and surprise them. It was tea time. I never even knocked on the door. Emmy was there, they were all there. God, did I get a hugging – three of them all at once, and Mum going on and on about how I was just skin and bone. Emmy wept buckets, and even Ossie had to dry his eyes. I'd never seen him do that before. And he called me a young scallywag for not warning them. I gave Emmy back her gold cross and said it had worked, which it had. But she wouldn't have it back, said I had to keep it. Back at Chelsea they treated me like a conquering hero. The war would be over soon enough now, six months, a year at the most, everyone knew it. They told me there'd always be a place for me back at the club when I'd finished with the army. I played a couple of practice games with some of the lads.

I wasn't as sharp as I had been – I wasn't strong enough to be sharp – but I could still tease them with my dribbling. I was soon out of puff though. I knew I'd have a lot of training, a lot of catching up to do if I was ever going to get back into the first team. But I'd do it. Nothing in the world was going to stop me from pulling on a Chelsea shirt again, not lousy Mr Hitler, nor his lousy war.

Home was difficult. They all knew I was going soon. So every day, every moment was precious, too precious for all of us. We couldn't be normal. And Joe's bed was still there across the room, and so was his box of cigarette cards on his shelf. I found myself talking to him even more now, sometimes aloud. I dreamt of him too, and I dreamt of Lucia and the shots echoing around the mountains.

I hate goodbyes, so I left a letter for each of

them and crept out of the house before dawn. Once I was on the train down to Dover, I was back in the army, back to left right, left right, saluting officers and polishing boots. So they sent me off to war for the second time. How I wish they never had.

I thought the fighting would be mostly done with by now, and so it was. But there were still so many wounded to look after – our lads, and Germans, and refugees. We were treating as many refugees as soldiers. I drove ambulances, swabbed down floors, made beds, buried people. That was when I first started to drink with the lads. I never had before. When the work was over we'd get together and drown our sorrows. The drink was cheap, and I discovered I had a bit of a taste for it. No more than that. Not then. Not yet.

We'd heard about the camps, concentration camps where they'd been exterminating Jews and anyone they didn't like; but I don't think any of us really believed it. You had to see it to believe it. But when I saw it, I still couldn't believe it. I didn't want to believe it.

As we drove in through the gates of Belsen in our convoy of ambulances, they came wandering towards us like ghosts, walking skeletons, some of them in striped pyjamas, some completely naked. They were staring at us as if we had come down from some other planet. The children

would come up to us and touch us, just to make sure we were real, I think. You couldn't call them children – more like little old people, skin and bone, nothing more, hardly living. They all moved slowly, shuffling. A strange silence hung over the place, and a horrible stench.

It was our job to do what we could for the sick, to get them eating again. As for the dying, we were usually too late.

We buried the dead in their thousands, in mass graves. You didn't want to look, but you had to. Once you've seen such things you can never forget them. They give out no medals for burying the dead, but if they did I'd have a chestful. There was one little boy I found in his bunk. I thought he was asleep. He was curled up with his thumb in his mouth. He was dead. I wrote home, but I couldn't tell them what I'd seen. I just couldn't.

When I left Belsen a few days later in a convoy of ambulances I was full of hate and anger, full of horror, and full of grief too for the little boy with his thumb in his mouth. I drank every evening now, drank to forget.

Thinking back, it was my fault. I should have kept to the track. Just a month or so after Belsen we were on our way to a refugee camp in Northern Germany somewhere. Four ambulances in the convoy, and I was driving the lead ambulance.

The military policeman directed us up a farm track and told us to keep on down to the end, and to keep on the track. But the farm track was impossible. Up to the axles in mud, we were slipping and sliding all over the place. The wheels just weren't gripping. I thought I'd get bogged down. The meadow to one side looked a better bet, so I left the farm track and drove along the edge of the field.

The next thing I knew I was in hospital. Later on they told me everything. The ambulance had hit a mine. I was lucky to be alive. I didn't feel lucky. I ached all over in every bone, and my left leg was agony. It had been crushed and broken in three places. I'd had an operation to put it right. The doctor was cheery, too cheery.

"Your leg's a bit of a mess, old chap," he said, "but you'll be up and walking on it soon enough.

It'll always be a bit stiff, and you won't be playing a lot of football, I'm afraid. But otherwise you'll be fine." Otherwise, you'll be fine. I've never forgotten those words. I wrote home a lot from my hospital bed, and told them what had happened, what the doctor had told me, how he didn't know what he was talking about, that I'd be playing football again just as soon as I got home. I wasn't fooling them, wasn't

fooling myself. I believed it. I really believed it.

A few weeks later they invalided me out, and I found myself walking down the Fulham Road, limping a little, and needing a stick, but happy as a lark. I'd surprise them all again. I turned into our street. Where my house had been there was no house. A V-2 bomb they said it was, the last one to fall on London. A direct hit. They'd all been buried in the churchyard next to Dad.

All I could think was – if only Emmy hadn't made me keep her gold cross, she might have been alive. They might all have lived.

I was there in Trafalgar Square the day the war ended. Everyone was so happy. I was swept along in the crowd up the Mall to Buckingham Palace. How they cheered, and sang, and danced, and hugged. And all I could do was watch. All I felt was emptiness. I did go back to Chelsea, but the doctor there said the same thing, I'd never play again.

They discharged me from the army. I had a demob suit and a disability pension and nothing to live for. I didn't feel sorry for myself. I didn't feel anything. One day I began to drink, and I just didn't stop. It's quite easy to fall apart, like going to sleep – you just drift into it.

For fifteen years I wandered the country,

sleeping rough. I went all over, up to the Highlands of Scotland, down to the tip of Cornwall. I lived in barns, in abandoned cottages, in bombed-out ruins, and once in a disused chapel. I had enough to get by. My disability pension bought me my drink, and I seemed to need less and less to eat. And the drink worked too. It numbed the sadness for me. I talked a lot to myself as I tramped the country lanes, and if not to myself, to Joe and Lucia and Mum and Emmy and Dad and Ossie. They were my companions on the road. I could make them real in my head – just so long as I drank enough.

But in all this time I never lost touch with Chelsea. I'd look out for them in the newspaper to see how they were doing. I knew the scores of every game, I knew where we were in the League, I knew the name of every player in the team.

When it was cold, I'd sit in libraries or in cafés – where it was warm – and read about Chelsea in the paper.

I'd grown a long straggly beard and I'm afraid I didn't wash too often either. The best thing I ever did was keep my old army great coat, a real life saver that was. There were some people who turned nasty at me – and I don't blame them, not really. I was drunk a lot of the time and I wasn't a pretty sight either, I know that. But the children were always kinder, the young ones anyway. If ever I kicked a football about with them they thought I was the bee's knees. I couldn't run about much of course, not any more, but I could still get up to a

few of my old tricks. They liked that, and so did I.

I never stayed in one place long enough to become a nuisance, nor long enough to get to know anyone. I just kept moving, over the next horizon, onto the next town. I spent the odd night in a police station, for vagrancy or drunkenness, but they were always happy to turf me out the next morning. I was never in any real trouble. But it was after a night in a police cell – up in Ipswich it was – that I decided to stop my wandering. It was early on a Sunday morning, and they'd just let me out. I was walking past the desk when I noticed the copper on duty had his paper open at the sports page. I asked him if Chelsea had won. They had.

"Lovely,"' I said.

"You a Chelsea supporter then?" he asked.

It turned out he was too. He'd grown up just across the river in Putney. He was Chelsea mad. On the strength of that he gave me a cup of tea and we talked Chelsea for an hour or more. And then he said it.

"Used to be a young lad there just before the war. Billy the Kid. Remember him? Just about the best we ever had. Never heard of him since, have you? Wonder what happened to him."

I didn't say anything.

"When I retire, three years from now," he went on. "I've got it all planned. I've told the wife. We're going to move back down to London and live right by the ground. I'll be right there on the spot for every match."

I set off for London the next day. I was there three years ahead of him. My travels were over.

I was back here in this park, my park, back where I belonged. I slept here on this bench for three nights, picked up my pension and went to the match on Saturday – against Fulham. We won two nil. The Shed End was roaring. I'd come home.

They need a ref out there. That's twice that poor lad's had his legs scythed away from under him. For two pins I'd go and volunteer myself. I'd better not. I've still got my banana to eat and my apple – got to keep healthy. It's nearly half past one. Perfect day for football. Bit of a breeze. God, I'd love to be playing.

I'd never dossed down in big cities. I liked to keep myself to myself and that's difficult in places like London. But I was lucky, I found the perfect place just off where we'd lived in Franklin Road. Someone had rebuilt our house – all very posh. But I was quite happy where I was in the basement of a dilapidated old house round the corner, all boarded up. It was dry, and there was even a bed down there, of sorts; and piles of old curtains which I used for blankets. I was still drinking, but now at least I had something to look forward to. I'd always put back enough of my pension money to buy my ticket. Every home match I was there at the Shed End. I was there when Stanley Matthews came down to Chelsea, 48 years old, and beat us, practically all by himself. Best of all I was there in May of 1963 when Bobby Tambling shot four goals past Portsmouth, and put us back up in Division One.

'Smelly Billy' they called me at the Shed End, but I didn't mind. I was one of them, one of the Chelsea family, and that made me feel good, better than I'd felt in a long, long time. When I talked to Joe now, down in my basement, I'd not be going on so much about my Belsen nightmares and my loneliness and all my miseries, I'd tell him more about how Chelsea was doing, who I thought Docherty should put in the team, and who he should leave out. But I still drank, drank hard. I knew I shouldn't, but I couldn't seem to stop myself.

The winter after Chelsea went up to Division One, my whole life changed. I'd been alone in my basement for three winters, and no one had bothered me. Then one day, I heard footsteps in the house above, and voices. I lay low and hoped they'd go away. But they didn't. I heard a key turn in the lock at the top of the basement stairs, and down they came. I thought of running, but I didn't see why I should. It was my place, my home. They were a young couple. They didn't seem to know what to say at first, just looked at me.

"I live here," I told them.

"Well that's all right," said the young lady, after a moment or two. "We've bought the place. We'll be doing it up ourselves. He can stay for a while, can't he, Jamie?"

The young man looked a bit doubtful. But then he shrugged and smiled.

"Why not?" he said.

So that's what happened. Jamie and Maddy moved in over my head, and did the place up. To begin with they left me be, and I left them be. But then from time to time Maddy would ask me up for a cup of tea and show me what they were doing. Nicest people you could ever hope to meet. I was happier then than I'd been in years. At nights I told Joe all about them, how they were looking after me, how I knew he'd like them. I began to give them a hand, carrying bricks and blocks and timber, doing a bit of cement work here and there, plastering, sweeping up, papering, whatever they wanted. We did it together, the three of us. And in the evenings sometimes we'd sit around on boxes up in their half-built sitting room and have pizzas and beer. They loved pizzas, lived on them. They were good times.

It was one evening after a late pizza that Maddy asked me where I'd come from, what had happened, how come they'd found me living rough in their basement. So I told them, told them everything from start to finish, I told them things I'd never told another soul, except Joe. When I finished Maddy put her arms round me and hugged me and cried. No one had done that since Emmy, since Mum.

But they didn't like it when I was drunk, I could see that. They always looked disappointed, but they never ticked me off. They just ignored me. And all the time the house was taking shape around us. Jamie often came with me to the matches – he was a Manchester United supporter to start with, but I didn't hold that against him. I gave him a Chelsea blue scarf for Christmas. I tied it round his neck and told him he was a Chelsea man now, whether he liked it or not. He liked it.

It was on the same Christmas Day that Maddy told me she was going to have a baby. I was so happy, happy for them, happy for me; but I could see that Jamie had something to say, and that somehow he didn't want to say it. He got round to it in the end.

"Thing is, Billy," he said, "I need a place to do my architectural work, my drawing. I was going to have the room at the top of the house, but now that will have to be the baby's room. I'll be needing the basement." My heart sank. I'd got used to the place, used to them, and now they wanted me to leave.

"When do you want me to go?" I asked them.

"We don't, you old silly. Of course we don't," said Maddy, laughing. "We've had an idea, haven't we, Jamie? Go on tell him, tell him, Jamie."

"Well, what if we built you a sort of cabin at the bottom of the garden?" said Jamie. "A place on your own. How'd that be?"

"Lovely," I said. "That'd be just lovely."

So up went the cabin and I went to live at the bottom of the garden. I had everything I needed – toilet, wash-basin, the lot. I only needed to come into the house for a bath. Maddy said it nicely. She said I was a bit sniffy and I should have a bath at least once a week.

But soon she was too busy with the new baby to bother about how sniffy I was.

They called him Sam, and I bought him a football. As soon as he was up and running I could see he was going to make a footballer. Before he was three I was kicking a tennis ball around with him in the garden. By five he could trap and turn and shoot, and with both feet too.

We always used a tennis ball, except at weekends, when I let him play with the big ball. I bought him his first pair of boots. I took him to his first match at Chelsea, got him a hat and scarf, and gave him a ride home on my shoulders. He loved coming down to my cabin for a story. He'd twiddle his fingers in my beard. He called me Uncle Billy and I thought the world of him.

Thinking about it now, I know it was Sam who stopped me drinking, Sam and Maddy. I would still get drunk from time to time, but then one day I did the unforgivable. Sam was about seven or eight by now, and at school down the road. One afternoon I found myself outside the school gates. I was drunk as a lord. They were all out in the playground. I saw Sam and he saw me. He waved and began to run across the playground towards me, and then he stopped. He saw the state of me and turned, and ran back indoors. I'd seen him recoil from me once or twice before. I'd promised myself I wouldn't ever get drunk when Sam was around. But I had.

No one came to my cabin that evening, and I was too ashamed to go and say sorry. The next morning Maddy came down the garden. I had never seen her angry before, but she was steaming angry now. She tore into me and told me exactly what she thought of me.

"If you want to go on drinking yourself to death, that's your business, but you're not going to do it in front of Sam. Do you understand that? If you ever, ever do that again, you're out! Out!" And then she looked around my cabin. "And look at this place. It's a mess. It's a tip. If you want to go on living here, you've got to clear it up, now."

And it was true. It was in a bit of a state. I'd become a bit of a jackdaw. In ten years I'd never thrown anything out.

"I've had just about

enough," she said. "I'm throwing everything into the garden, the whole lot. And while you're about it, you can shave off that filthy beard, and have a bath, and cut your nails."

She set about emptying my whole cabin into the garden, scattering everything all over the grass. By the time she had finished she was in tears. I had to have a big bonfire, she said, and burn the

lot. I chucked out all my empty bottles, shaved off my beard, had a bath and cut my nails. That evening sitting round the kitchen table they came to an agreement with me. They were both very stern. They would let me stay, but only under certain conditions. I would be allowed two beers a day, one in the morning and one in the evening. They would bring it to me. I was never ever to buy a drink for myself again. I had to do my teeth twice a day, have a bath once a day and keep my clothes clean. I agreed, and I stayed. Best thing I ever did. I kept the garden tidy for them, looked after the house, even did a bit of the cooking – I wasn't bad either. And little Sam was my pride and joy. Every day we'd be out in the park practising. I taught him all the skills I knew, trained him so he could run as fast as a whippet – he was small like me. I taught him to be tough as a terrier too. He was soon scoring goals for his school, out on the wing, the right wing, and he was good enough now to go for training at Chelsea. At seventeen he was playing in the Chelsea Reserves, and I was there seven years ago with Maddy and Jamie when he ran out for Chelsea for the first time. Proudest day of my life that was. Chelsea lost, but I didn't care.

Better not lose this afternoon. Come on, Billy, up you get. You'd best be on your way. Kick-off won't wait for you. Back to my room first and get into my finery. Maddy says I look good in my scarlet uniform, a knock out, she says. The old knee's a bit stiff today. It's always better when I get walking. My bottom's numb. Ruddy hard, that bench.

Who knows what causes these things – too much excitement maybe, but the next day, I had a bit of a stroke. Nothing much, the doctor said, but I'd have to take it easy. It affected my eyesight more than anything else – all the peripheries are still a bit fuzzy. I'd have been quite happy staying where I was in the cabin, but it was winter and Maddy wouldn't hear of it. For a while I found myself living again in the basement in Jamie's studio. But we all knew that couldn't go on for ever. It was Jamie who found a way out of it, a way that suited us all perfectly – the Royal Hospital Chelsea: a sort of retirement home for old soldiers. He'd found out all about it. It was only just down the road. They had over 300 old soldiers in there, all beautifully looked after, everything an old fellow like me could wish for.

"You're an old soldier," he said. "And you've got a disability pension, so you'd qualify. I've checked. All you have to do is have an interview."

To be honest I wasn't all that happy with the idea at first. But when I saw the place I changed my mind. I'd have my own cubicle, three good meals a day and everything provided. And best of all, it wasn't that far from Chelsea Football Club. I had my interview with the Adjutant Colonel and the Captain of Invalides. I liked them and they seemed to like me. I had a three-day stay, sleeping there and eating there, just to see how I got on. I loved every minute of it. I had a lot of fellows to talk to and I got on well with them, but I did miss home and Sam and Jamie and Maddy. I wasn't at all sure I wanted to stay there for good and all.

I was sitting in the sunshine trying to work it all out when someone sat down beside me – one of the pensioners in his scarlet uniform. He was looking at me, studying me. After a while he said, "Were you a prisoner in Italy during the war?"

"Yes," I said. I couldn't see him very well with the sun behind him.

"It's Robbie, Billy. Don't you remember me?"

We did a lot of thumping of shoulders, and we

shed a tear or two as well. That decided me. Within a month I moved in and became a Chelsea Pensioner. I'd seen them about in their scarlet coats – some of them always come to watch Chelsea – and always thought how fine they looked. Now I'm one of them. And what a life of Riley I have. I paint a bit, when my eyes

aren't too fuzzy, and I play a lot of bowls with Robbie. He hasn't changed, not one bit. He still looks after me as if I was his little brother. And he soon spread it around who I'd been when I was a young man. I can't think why, but he's really proud of me. So now everyone calls me 'Billy the Kid' again. Funny how things come around.

I eat like a horse, go home every Sunday for lunch to see the family, and do just what I like – but I never ever have more than two beers a day. And every home game I'm there down at the Shed End at Chelsea watching Sam play. He's the best winger they've ever had, and he's played twenty-five times for England. He's not perfect though. Without telling me he went and told them who I was down at the club and they made a bit of a fuss of me. I was made an honorary life member and given my seat at the Shed End free for the rest of my life. It was in all the newspapers. So down at Chelsea they all know who I am now. I'm quite famous in a sort of a way, and I like that. In fact, I like that a lot.

I can hear the crowd inside the ground now, Joe. The streets are packed, like a river of blue all flowing towards Chelsea. They're a rowdy mob, always were, but friendly.

Something's up, Joe. I don't know what, but something's up. That Gianluca Vialli – I told you about him, best player-manager there ever was, Italian fellow, not much hair – well, he's just come out to meet me. He just shook my hand. I'm not sure what's going on. He's taking me down to the players' dressing room, he says. Always the same smell in a dressing room – embrocation, sweat, boots. They're all clapping me, Joe. They're all here, all my heroes, Zola, Jody, Wisey,

Le Saux, Desailly, Sam, and they're singing me Happy Birthday. Sam's given me the match programme. I'm on the front cover! It was Sam. Sam set this whole thing up, the beggar. I've got tears in my eyes and they won't stop coming. Zola's given me the match ball. They want me to lead the team out onto the field. I'm going to be walking out there, Joe, and you're going to be with me all the way, down the tunnel and out into the light, out into the noise. And they're chanting, Joe, they're chanting,

"Billy, Billy the Kid! Billy, Billy the Kid!"

Jamie's here and Maddy, and Robbie too. They all knew about it. So-and-sos! All a conspiracy, a lovely conspiracy. It's a long walk out, but I want it to last for ever and ever. They're singing Happy Birthday now, and they've got me up on the big screens.

RESTAURANT
WIZARD
AUTOGLASS
AUTOGLASS
CARLING

I'll do a fancy dribble around Wisey, and then I'll go back to my seat in the Shed End. I can still dribble a little, enough to make them cheer.

Are you listening, Joe? Are you watching? Maybe you're proud of me again now. I hope so.

AUTHOR'S NOTES

The Battle of the Somme

One of the most bloody battles of the First World War (1914–1918). In July 1916 after a long artillery barrage the British Army attacked the German trenches on the Somme River in Northern France. But the Germans were well dug in, well prepared. The British marched forward into a hail of bullets. On the first day of the battle the British Army lost 60,000 men, killed or wounded, the worst losses ever suffered by the British Army in a single day. Such bravery and such disasters caused one German general to say of the British soldiers that they were "lions led by donkeys".

Adolf Hitler

Founder and leader of the National Socialist Party (the Nazi Party), he was elected Chancellor of Germany in 1933. Very soon he assumed dictatorial powers and began to build up the German armed forces. It was his invasions of the neighbouring states of Austria, Czechoslovakia and then Poland that led Britain to declare war on Germany in September 1939. Later, his invasion of the Soviet Union (the Russian Empire) brought that country into the war. When Japan, an ally of Germany, attacked the United States, the war became truly global. It is thought that over 30 million people died in the Second World War. Hitler himself committed suicide in a bunker in Berlin in May of 1945 as the city was being overwhelmed by the Soviet army.

The 'phoney war'

For some months after the declaration of war on September 3rd 1939, very little seemed to happen. It was in 1940 with Hitler's invasions of France, Belgium, Holland, Denmark and Norway, and with the beginning of aerial bombardment of Britain, that the war began to feel like a real war.

Dunkirk

The Second World War (1939–1945) began with a series of defeats for the Allies. When the Germans invaded France and Belgium and Holland in the summer of 1940, their advance was so swift that they rolled the Allies back to the English Channel within weeks. At Dunkirk, the remnants of the Allied armies were trapped. The only way out was the sea. Over a quarter of a million men were evacuated by an armada of little ships sent over from England; but thousands were killed on the beaches, or taken prisoner.

Tobruk

Here, in this port on the North African coast in June 1942, yet again a British army found itself driven back by German tanks. Thousands of soldiers were cut off and captured.

POW Camps

Prisoner-of-war camps were set up to confine

captured soldiers of all sides. Conditions were often very harsh, and the food poor and scarce. Many soldiers spent five long years shut up in these camps.

The Land Army

With so many farmers and agricultural workers away fighting in the war, and with the ever-increasing need for home-grown food (so many ships were being sunk that the supply of imported food was all but halted), many women volunteered to go out in the country and work on the land – the Land Army.

Resistance Fighters

In every occupied country in Europe groups of resistance fighters sprang up. In the south of

France they were known as the 'Maquis', in Italy 'Partisans'. Both harried the German occupying forces in any way they could, and many thousands of resistance fighters lost their lives.

Italy and the War

In 1939 the Italians under their dictator Mussolini allied themselves with the Germans under Hitler. However, in 1943 the Italians removed Mussolini from power, signed an armistice and came out of the war. Hitler at once invaded them from the north and soon occupied all of Italy. The Allied armies landed in the south to drive the German army out, and in the summer of 1944 at last liberated the capital city, Rome.

The V-2 Rocket

In 1945, with the war coming to an end, Hitler tried one last time to snatch victory from defeat. In order to terrify Britain into submission, he launched a guided missile attack on London – V-2 rockets or flying bombs. They did great damage, but for Hitler it was too little too late.

Belsen

As Europe was being liberated by the Russians from the east, from the west by the Allies, dreadful discoveries were made – concentration camps where the Germans had systematically set out to exterminate Jews, gypsies, the mentally ill, anyone they considered undesirable. Millions of men, women and children perished in these camps, some in gas chambers, some by deliberate neglect, by starvation and disease. It was the British army that came across Bergen-Belsen concentration camp in north-west Germany. Here they discovered 10,000 unburned bodies and the mass graves of 40,000 more. Of the 30,000 still alive when the soldiers arrived, most were too weak to survive, and died soon after. Anne Frank died in Bergen-Belsen in 1945 only weeks before the camp was liberated.

The Royal Hospital, Chelsea

Founded by Charles II in the seventeenth century, the Royal Hospital houses and cares for 350 Chelsea Pensioners, all old soldiers. If you go to Chelsea you may see them walking the streets in their scarlet coats. They wear scarlet coats as their best or 'dress' uniforms, and blue coats for everyday wear. Some of them go to watch Chelsea play on Saturdays at Stamford Bridge. One of them, I noticed, sometimes sits all on his own behind the goal at the Shed End.

The Royal Army Medical Corps

The army regiment whose task it is to care for wounded and sick soldiers. This task extends, of course, to looking after civilians and refugees caught up in war.

Chelsea Football Club

Chelsea Football Club has played at Stamford Bridge ground since it was formed in 1905.

The club gives Chelsea Pensioners 8 free seats in the Directors' Box for every home game. The Pensioners draw lots for the tickets but one old soldier who wants to see every game has his own season ticket at the Shed End.

And lastly…

'Toad in the hole'

Sausages in batter roasted in the oven. My favourite meal when I was little. Yummy.
Try it!

Chelsea
Liverpool